5-MINUTE KINDNESS STORIES

Random House 🏠 New York

CONTENTS

WE LOVE FRIENDSHIP DAY!

By Matt Huntley

Based on the teleplay "Pups Save Friendship Day"
by Michael Stokes

Illustrated by MJ Illustrations

It was Friendship Day in Adventure Bay, and the PAW Patrol pups were getting ready to celebrate. Skye and Rocky decorated the Lookout, and the rest of the pups made cards for everyone in town.

"I love Friendship Day," Skye said as she hung a colorful banner. "It's just so . . . friendly!"

"Paint cannons ready!" Marshall announced. He squirted the pup-shaped cards with different colors. "An ocean-blue card for Cap'n Turbot, apple-red for Farmer Yumi, and broccoli-green for Mr. Porter."

When the paint was dry, Chase put the cards into envelopes, and Zuma licked the stamps. "Yuck," Zuma said with a groan. "I wish we had liver-flavored stamps."

Marshall loaded the cards onto Rubble's Digger. On their way to give the cards to Mr. Postman to deliver, they passed a spooky house.

"A friend of a friend of a friend told me a creepy critter lives there," Rubble whispered.

Something scratched at the old fence, and the pups sped away.

The pups found Mr. Postman just as Mayor Humdinger from Foggy Bottom walked up the street. A mischievous kitten from the Kit-tastrophe Crew was at the mayor's side.

"We have some friendship cards that need delivering, too," said the mayor.

Suddenly, the kitten launched a flurry of hat-shaped cards at Mr. Postman, and he fell over!

"My ankle!" he exclaimed. "How will I *dee*-liver all these cards to those *dee*-serving folks?"

This was a job for the PAW Patrol!

The pups went to work delivering the cards. Skye carried some to the mountains. Zuma took some out to sea. Marshall handled the rest.

Marshall's first stop was Hootie the owl's tree—which was next to the spooky house he'd passed earlier.
He climbed up the tree—and slipped! The bag of cards fell into the yard.

Marshall needed to get the cards—but what was that noise? Was Rubble right? *Was* there a creepy critter on the other side of the fence? Just then, a mysterious shadow slid over the grass. Marshall jumped back into his truck and called Ryder.

"Hang tight, Marshall," Ryder said. "I'll send Rubble to lift the bag out with his crane."

Rubble was there in a flash. He backed his Digger up to the fence and lowered the crane's claw to lift up the cards. But just as he was about to snag the bag, the creepy critter grabbed it and darted into the house!

"Oh, no—now what?" Marshall asked.

"Maybe we could knock on the door and ask for the bag back?" Rubble suggested.

The two pups walked slowly up the path to the front door and knocked.

The door creaked open.
"Hello!" said an older woman, smiling. "I'm Miss Marjorie."
The pups sighed with relief. Miss Marjorie wasn't scary at all!
"What about the creepy critter that lives here?" Rubble asked.
"You mean Maynard?" Miss Marjorie said. "He's just a
grouchy old raccoon. Maynard wouldn't hurt a fly . . . or a pup!"

Ryder caught up with the pups at Miss Marjorie's house. "Wouldn't making a new friend be the best way to celebrate Friendship Day?" Marshall asked.

Rubble and Ryder agreed, so Ryder invited Miss Marjorie to help him deliver the last of the cards.

Then they all drove to the big Friendship Day party at the Adventure Bay town hall. Friends new and old were there—Miss Marjorie, the pups, Mr. Postman, and even Mayor Humdinger.

Everyone agreed that Adventure Bay was definitely the friendliest town around!

TRACK THAT MONKEY!

By Casey Neumann

Based on the teleplay "Pups Save Big Hairy"
by James Backshall and Jeff Sweeney

Illustrated by MJ Illustrations

One day, the PAW Patrol were in the jungle helping their friends
Carlos and Tracker give the monkeys their yearly checkups.
Tracker used his magnifying glass to examine Mandy the monkey.
"I'm ready to take Mandy's X-ray!" said Marshall.

Mandy put her face behind Marshall's scanner. The image of her bones surprised the other monkeys, and they started running in circles.

"Uh-oh! How do we calm them down?" asked Rocky.

"Scratch their backs!" said Carlos. "Monkeys love that!"

Rocky extended the claw from his Pup Pack and went to work scratching backs. The monkeys quickly relaxed.

"Looks like you've made some new friends, Rocky!" Marshall yelped.

Just then, a giant monkey named Big Hairy peeked around a rock and saw Rocky's back scratcher. He really wanted to have his back scratched!

Chase and Zuma arrived, back from searching the jungle.

"We looked all over, but we didn't find any more monkeys who need a checkup," said Chase.

Carlos decided it was time to close the monkey checkup center. He thanked the PAW Patrol for their help.

Marshall invited Tracker to come back with the pups for a visit.

The pups happily scampered into the PAW Patroller as Carlos and the monkeys waved goodbye.

The PAW Patroller rumbled along the jungle road. Suddenly, big bunches of bananas landed on the roof.

"¿*Escucharon?*" Tracker asked. "Did anyone else hear that?"

Ryder and the pups didn't see anything outside.

"Probably just some bumps in the road," Ryder suggested. They didn't realize that Big Hairy was riding on the roof of their vehicle!

As the PAW Patroller rolled into town, Big Hairy saw the giant cup on top of Mr. Porter's lemonade stand. He leaped from the vehicle onto the stand's roof. He rubbed his back against the huge cup—and it broke loose and crashed to the ground!

Next, Big Hairy ran to the statue of Chickaletta in front of city hall and rubbed his back against it. The statue fell over with a thud!

The giant monkey quickly ran off to find something else to scratch his back on.

Mayor Goodway saw the trouble Big Hairy was causing and called the PAW Patrol. They raced to the rescue and found Big Hairy outside Mr. Porter's market. Rocky used his catapult to launch bananas at the monkey. Tracker tried to lure him away by pulling the banana-filled wagon with his cables.

The giant monkey wasn't interested.

"Why isn't he going after the bananas?" Rocky asked.

That was when Ryder noticed that Big Hairy was scratching his fur and pointing at Rocky's claw. He understood that the big monkey wasn't just causing trouble, he had a problem and the PAW Patrol needed to help him.

Big Hairy made his way to the Lookout and climbed to the top of the tower.

Chase used his megaphone to check on Rocky.

"How are you doing up there, Rocky?" he called.

"I'm okay," Rocky replied. "But I'm getting tired of scratching!"

After a moment, Ryder had an idea!

Skye swooped in and nudged Big Hairy away from the edge of the roof. Then Zuma moved the periscope up and down from the control room to scratch Big Hairy's back.

He was so relaxed, he let go of Rocky.

Skye dangled a bunch of bananas just out of Big Hairy's reach, then slowly lowered them to the roof. The giant monkey climbed down the Lookout and followed Skye to the PAW Patroller.

Everything was back to normal . . . except Big Hairy's back was still itchy!

Rocky ran over to Big Hairy and gave him a giant back scratcher. "I made you something to remember me by!" Rocky exclaimed. Big Hairy was thrilled. He grabbed his new back scratcher and hopped onto the roof of the PAW Patroller. He was ready to head back to the jungle! He had only acted out because he was itchy and uncomfortable, and his friends found a way to help him.

Ryder asked Robo Dog to take Big Hairy home, and soon the PAW Patroller began to roll away. Everyone said goodbye to the big monkey.

Big Hairy had given the pups a busy day, but Ryder understood that their new friend had had a problem. They took the time to learn what was wrong and figured out how to help him.

"And remember," Ryder called, "whenever you have an itch, just *ooka-ooka* for help!"

The pups laughed and cheered.

LET'S VISIT THE DOCTOR

By Francis Xavier

Illustrated by Nate Lovett

One morning, the PAW Patrol was finishing a mission in Adventure Bay. Ryder received a message from Everest on his PupPad.

"I'm worried about Jake," she said. "He seems a little sick."

"He should go to the doctor," Ryder said.

"That's what I told him to do," Everest replied. "But he says he's too busy."

"We'll be right there," Ryder said.

The team raced to Jake's cabin. When they got there, they found their friends on the front porch. Marshall took Jake's temperature. "Looks like you're a little warm. You should see a doctor," he said.

"I'll go to the doctor when I have time," Jake answered. "Right now, I'm too busy. I have to fix these steps and move some rocks that rolled down the mountain. And then—*AH-CHOO!*"

Jake nodded slowly. "I do feel a little tired and achy."
"If you're feeling ill," Everest said, "you should see Dr. Duval.
He'll help you feel better and make sure you don't get even sicker."
"But what about everything I need to do?" Jake asked.

"The pups can help while you go to the doctor," Ryder said.

"Yeah, I can fix that broken step!" Rocky exclaimed as a hammer popped out of his PupPack.

"I can move those rocks that fell," Rubble said. "Rubble on the double!"

"Are you sure that's not too much trouble for you?" Jake asked. "That's sounds like a lot of work, and I'm think I'm feeling bet—*AH-CHOO!*"

Ryder smiled. "Don't worry about it. That's what friends do for each other. We're always ready to help someone, especially someone who is sick. Everest, Marshall, and I can help get you to the doctor!" he said.

Ryder, Jake, and the pups arrived at Dr. Duval's office.
They opened the door and stepped into the waiting room.
They sat down until it was Jake's turn to see the doctor.
There were books and puzzles to help pass the time.

EAT
HEA

Jake even saw Cap'n Turbot.

"Are you feeling sick, too?" Jake asked him.

"I'm feeling fit and fine, my friend," Cap'n Turbot said. "Just coming in for my yearly checkup."

"It's important to see the doctor at least once a year," Ryder said. "Even if you feel okay."

Jake didn't have to wait very long. Dr. Duval opened the door to the examination room.

"Hi, Jake," he said. "Are you and your friends ready to come in?"

Jake sat on the examination table and took off his shirt.
"How are you feeling?" Dr. Duval asked.
"A little sniffly and tired," Jake replied. "I just have a cold."
"Well, let's do the exam, just to be sure," Dr. Duval said.
"This will be really quick and easy."

Dr. Duval put on his stethoscope.

"This is so I can hear inside your body," said Dr. Duval. "Take a deep breath. Now let it out. Good. Everything sounds healthy."

After that, Dr. Duval took Jake's temperature with a thermometer.

"Ninety-eight point six degrees is normal," he said. "But you're a little warmer than that. You have a bit of a fever."

"I knew it!" Marshall announced with a smile.

The doctor also checked Jake's throat. "Say 'Ahhh.'"

"Ahhhhh," Jake echoed. Then he added, *"CHOO!"*

He had sneezed again!

"Well, we're all done," Dr. Duval said, making some notes in his folder. "You were right. You do have a small cold. But it's good you came in. If you don't take care of yourself, small colds can get big."

The doctor told Jake to get lots of rest and eat some hot soup.

When Jake returned to the lodge, the step was fixed and the rocks had been moved.

"Wow, you pups did great work," Jake said, sniffling. "Thank you."

Just then, Skye came in for a landing with a brown paper bag.

"Watch out!" she said. "I've got some hot soup from Mr. Porter's restaurant."

Jake put on his coziest pajamas, wrapped himself in a blanket, and enjoyed a bowl of soup.

"I was silly to think I didn't have time to go to the doctor," he said. "Especially when I have such great friends who can help me out."

"There's always time to go to the doctor," Ryder said.
"Yeah, you should go for a visit if you don't feel good," said Everest.
"And make sure to get regular checkups, too!" said Marshall.
"And if you ever think you're too busy . . . ," Rubble said, smiling.
"Just yelp for help!" finished Jake.

SEA PATROL TO THE RESCUE!

By Francis Xavier

Based on the teleplay "Pups Save a Baby Octopus"
by James Beckshall and Jeff Sweeney

Illustrated by Nate Lovett

One sunny morning, the PAW Patrol were at their new Beach Tower headquarters. Mayor Goodway had asked the pups to be Adventure Beach's new lifeguard rescue team. She wanted them on duty during her luau that afternoon.

"We'll be the Sea Patrol," Ryder announced. "But before you can save anyone, you'll have to earn your lifeguard badges."

"Ready, set, get wet!" barked Zuma.

For the lifeguard test, the pups didn't rescue a person. They took turns swimming through a course of floating buoys and rescuing a pineapple named Mr. Prickly! One by one, each pup earned a badge . . . until it was Rocky's turn.

Instead of swimming, Rocky jumped from buoy to buoy, then threw a life ring around Mr. Prickly. He pulled the pineapple in and hopped back to shore without getting wet!

"Cool rescue technique," Ryder said. "But if you want to earn your lifeguard badge, you have to swim."

Rocky was happy to be a land guard.

Ryder realized his friend didn't like to get wet and might have been a little afraid of swimming. He didn't want to push too hard or embarrass him, so he tried to be encouraging.

"I know you can do this," said Ryder. "If you don't feel up to it now, you can try again later."

Meanwhile, Cap'n Turbot was out at sea feeding Wally the Walrus. "Here's some more juicy jellyfish jerky," he said. He didn't realize that a baby octopus was stuck to the side of his chum bucket.

Suddenly, the water started churning, and Cap'n Turbot's boat, the *Flounder*, began to rock. Giant tentacles reached out of the waves and wrapped around the boat.

"Great gushing geysers—I need the PAW Patrol!" Cap'n Turbot exclaimed, and he called Ryder.

Ryder, Rubble, Zuma, and Marshall boarded the *Sea Patroller* and sped to the troubled *Flounder*. Zuma and Rubble hit the waves in their new sea vehicles.

Zuma tried to pull the tentacles off Cap'n Turbot's boat with his vehicle's mechanical arms, but the sea monster was too strong.

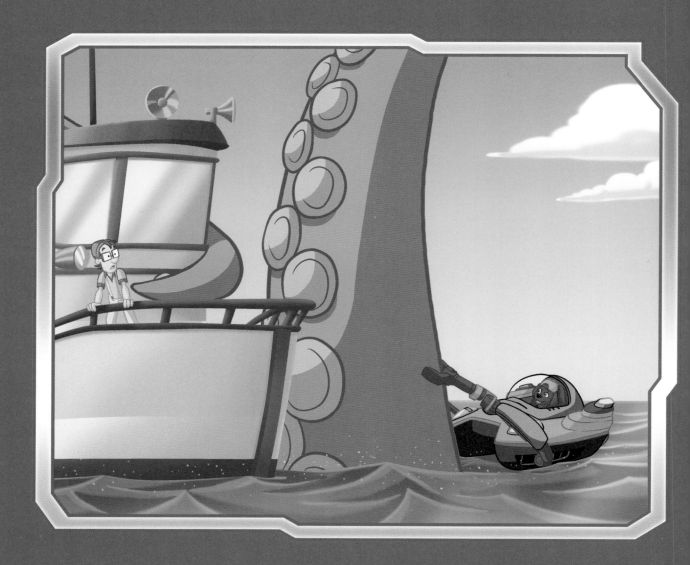

Ryder had an idea. He told Robo Dog to sound the *Sea Patroller*'s horn. *BWAAAAAAAA!*

The startled sea monster released the *Flounder* and slid back below the ocean's surface.

"Hooray!" everyone cheered.

But just then, the *Flounder* started to sink— and Cap'n Turbot was still on it!

Marshall put on his scuba gear, dove into the water, and went to work. He found the sunken *Flounder* and started pumping it full of air from his tanks. The boat floated up toward the surface.

As Marshall watched the boat rise, something shiny caught his eye. Was it undersea treasure?

He picked it up with his mechanical claw and shook it. "It's a baby rattle!" he exclaimed.

Meanwhile, Cap'n Turbot was back on Adventure Beach trying to cheer himself up at Mayor Goodway's luau. But while he looked for something to eat, the baby octopus jumped off him and landed on Mayor Humdinger's head!

"Help!" the mayor shouted. "Get it off!"

Just then, the sea monster rose out of the waves! Skye took to the air with her parasail to distract it.

When Ryder arrived, he saw that the sea monster was actually an octopus—and it was squinting. "It's looking for something, but it can't see very well."

"Well, keep it away from me," muttered Mayor Humdinger. "I don't want that on my head, too!"

Then Ryder realized the giant octopus was the little octopus's mother. "We need to get that baby back to its mom!"

But first they had to get the baby off Mayor Humdinger's head. Marshall remembered the rattle he'd found and started shaking it.

The baby octopus reached for the toy . . . but because Mayor Humdinger couldn't see, he accidentally knocked the rattle into the ocean!

Someone had to get that rattle!

"I can find it with my metal detector," said Rocky.

"Are you sure, Rocky?" Ryder asked. "You'll have to swim and get wet."

"If getting wet will help the baby octopus get back to its mom, I can do it!" Rocky declared. He extended his metal detector, bravely dove into the water, and found the rattle!

Shaking the toy, Zuma boarded the *Sea Patroller* with Ryder and headed away from the beach. The little octopus followed the rattling noise . . . and the mother followed her baby. Out in the deep water, the mother and baby found each other and hugged.

Ryder understood that the big octopus wasn't trying to be mean and scary, she had lost her baby and was worried. He realized there was a way to help her. He quickly made eyeglasses out of two punch bowls from the luau. Now the mother could always find her baby.

Back on the beach, everyone cheered for the pups—and for Cap'n Turbot's newly repaired *Flounder*.

"Thank you, PAW Patrol," said Mayor Goodway. "You saved the beach *and* the party!"

Ryder knew there was one particular hero who needed recognition. Rocky had been scared of getting wet, but his friends gave him time to face his fears.

"I think Rocky deserves the biggest thank-you," said Ryder. "He got wet to save the day and earned this." Ryder pinned a lifeguard badge to Rocky's vest. All the pups howled and hoorayed for their brave friend!

ICE TEAM

By Matt Huntley

Based on the teleplay "The New Pup"
by Ursula Ziegler-Sullivan

Illustrated by MJ Illustrations

One sunny day, the PAW Patrol was getting ready for a trip to see their friend Jake at the ice fields.

Suddenly, there was a loud roar, and a big truck rolled up.

"Presenting the PAW Patroller!" Ryder announced. "It's a Lookout on wheels. It can take us anywhere!"

A door opened in the side and a mechanical dog hopped out.

"Robo Dog will be our driver!"

As Ryder was showing the pups around the PAW Patroller, Jake called.

"Hey, Jake! How are the ice fields?" Ryder asked.

"Amazing!" Jake declared. "Take a look!"

The screen showed snowy hills and an icy river.

Just then, Jake slipped on the ice, and the pups could
hear him yell, "My phone! My maps! All my stuff!"
Jake's equipment had splashed into the icy river!

"Jake's in big trouble!" Rubble exclaimed.
"Pups, get your vehicles," Ryder said.
The PAW Patroller's back door opened and a ramp came out. The pups quickly drove their vehicles aboard. Robo Dog started the engine and the PAW Patroller rolled into action.

At the ice fields, Jake was trying to get his
backpack out of the water. But the riverbank was so
icy that he began to slide in! Luckily,
a husky pup pulled him out.
  "Sweet save!" Jake said, then introduced himself.
  "My name's Everest!" the pup exclaimed.
"I rescued someone! I've always wanted
to do a real rescue."

"We should probably get going," Everest said. "A storm's rolling in. I wouldn't want to lose my first real rescue in a blizzard. We can wait it out in my igloo. To get there, we can do this. . . ."

Everest flopped onto her belly and slid down the hill.

"Belly-bogganing!" Jake shouted, taking off after her. "Look out below!"

The two new friends slid along on the ice, zooming past some penguins.

When the PAW Patroller reached the ice fields, the snow was falling hard. The team started to look for Jake. They quickly found his frozen phone and pack. "This means Jake doesn't have any supplies," Ryder said. Then he noticed something in the snow. "Are those tracks?"

Chase gave the tracks a sniff. "That's Jake, all right! And he's got another pup with him."

"Those tracks should lead us to Jake," Ryder announced. "Let's follow them."

As Chase followed the tracks on the ground,
Skye took to the frosty air. "This pup's got to fly!"

Everest and Jake came to a narrow bridge that stretched across a deep, dark ravine. "My igloo is just across that ice bridge," Everest said.

"Will it hold us?" Jake asked.

"I hope so," the husky replied. "It's the only way to get over."

As they walked across, they heard a terrible cracking noise. The ice bridge was breaking!

Just as the bridge collapsed, Skye swooped in, catching Jake and Everest with a rope. But before she had carried them to the other side of the ravine, the rope broke.

"Jump!" Jake yelled.

Everest landed on a ledge, but Jake missed it.
He caught the edge with his fingers and dangled
over the dark ravine.

"Don't worry!" Everest yelled. "I've got you!"
She snagged Jake's sleeve and pulled him to safety.
"Yes—two rescues in one day!"

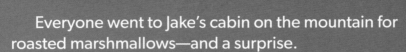

Everyone went to Jake's cabin on the mountain for roasted marshmallows—and a surprise.

"Everest," Jake said, "I could use a smart pup like you to help out on the mountain."

"And for saving Jake and showing great rescue skills," Ryder added, "I'd like to make you an official member of the PAW Patrol!"

"This is the best day ever!" Everest exclaimed, and all the pups cheered.

THE PUPS SAVE THE BUNNIES

By Matt Huntley

Based on the teleplay by Ursula Ziegler-Sullivan

Illustrated by MJ Illustrations

It was a sunny day, and Mr. Porter was visiting Farmer Yumi to get some carrots for his market. But there was a problem. . . . The carrots were disappearing into the dirt!

"These carrots are growing backward!" Mr. Porter exclaimed.

But Farmer Yumi knew what was really happening—bunnies were eating her carrots.

This was a job for the PAW Patrol!

Ryder called the PAW Patrol to the Lookout and told them about the bunnies.

"We need to move the bunnies to a field where they'll be safe and won't eat Farmer Yumi's carrots. Rubble, I'll need your shovel so we can find the bunnies' tunnels."

"Rubble on the double!" he yelped.

"And, Chase, I'll need your megaphone and herding skills to round up the bunnies," Ryder continued.

"Chase is on the case!" the police pup exclaimed.

Ryder, Rubble, and Chase raced to Farmer Yumi's Farm. "Let's dig in!" Rubble said, and he started digging for the bunny tunnels. "I think I found something!" he shouted a few moments later. "In fact, I found *two* somethings!"

Ryder needed a way to carry the two bunnies from the
farm. He called Rocky and Skye on his Pup Pad. "Rocky,
can you get some old kennel cages so Skye can fly them
here?"

"Don't lose it—reuse it!" Rocky said.

"And I'll be there in two shakes of a bunny's tail,"
Skye added.

Skye arrived with the kennel cages, and Chase started
herding the bunnies into them.

But the busy day wasn't over yet! When Mr. Porter returned to his market, he found some furry-tailed surprises in the box of vegetables he'd brought from the farm. This was another job for the PAW Patrol!

The team sped to Mr. Porter's market.

Ryder had a plan for how to collect the bunnies. "I need some of your delicious carrot cake, Mr. Porter," he said.

Ryder set the cake on the ground, and all the bunnies bounded over to it. "Now we need your net, Chase!"

Chase launched his net over the bunnies, and Ryder carefully scooped them up.

Skye carried the last of the bunnies to their new home in the faraway field. As soon as Ryder opened the kennel cages, the little bunnies bounced into the grass and began to happily munch on flowers.

"Bye-bye, bunnies," Skye said. "I'm going to miss you."

When Skye returned to the Lookout, she realized she wasn't alone—a bunny had stowed away with her! "Can we keep her?"

"We can handle *one* bunny," Ryder said.

"Ryder, you're the best," Skye cheered as the pups welcomed their new furry friend.

CHASE'S LOOSE TOOTH

Adapted by Casey Neumann

Based on the episode "Pups Save a Toof"
by Ursula Ziegler-Sullivan

Illustrated by MJ Illustrations

One sunny day, Chase, Marshall, Zuma, and Rubble were playing tug-of-war.

Suddenly, Chase lost his grip and fell backward with a thud. "Ouch!" he yelped. That was when he felt his tooth wiggle!

"What's wrong, Chase?" asked Marshall.

"My tooth ith looth!" Chase said.

"Loose teeth are awesome!" Zuma exclaimed. "When you put them under your pillow, the tooth fairy leaves you something great!"

But Chase wasn't convinced. He went to his doghouse to lie down.

Ryder joined the pups and peeked in on Chase.
"You should really have the dentist take a look at that," he said.
Chase was scared.
"There is nothing to be afraid of," Ryder reassured him.
"The dentist will make sure your teeth are healthy and strong."

Meanwhile, across town, Alex was playing in his tree house. It was time for his checkup at the dentist.

His grandpa, Mr. Porter, called for him to come down. But Alex didn't want to go.

Using the back of a hammer, Alex pried off the top few steps of his ladder.

"A broken ladder?" Mr. Porter said. "Guess I'll have to borrow one to help get you down."

"Yes!" Alex whispered to himself. "Now there won't be enough time to go to the dentist!"

Mr. Porter reached for his phone. "I bet the PAW Patrol can get you down in a jiffy," he said with a smile.

The team arrived on the scene. Marshall backed up his fire truck and raised the ladder high. But Alex still refused to come down from the tree house.

"I'm scared of the dentist," he admitted.

"That's okay. Everyone is scared of something," Ryder explained.

"Not you and the PAW Patrol," Alex said.

That gave Ryder an idea.
"If I can get the PAW Patrol to do things they're scared of,
will you go to the dentist?"
Alex agreed to Ryder's deal.

Ryder went first. He asked Mr. Porter to bring him the one thing that scared him the most— Brussels sprouts!

Mr. Porter handed Ryder a fresh Brussels sprout. Ryder chewed it up and swallowed it down.

"See? That wasn't so bad," he said to Alex.

"Rocky, what are you scared of?" Ryder asked.

"Um, well . . . uh . . . water," Rocky said. He asked Marshall to spray him with his fire hose. *Splash!*

"Eww, now I'm gonna have that wet-pup smell!" Rocky whined. Alex chuckled.

"And Rubble is afraid of spiders," Ryder said, picking up a spider with a stick. The spider traveled down a thread to Rubble's nose!

It sat there for a few seconds and then crawled away. Rubble was just fine!

"Marshall is scared of flying," Ryder said.

Skye locked Marshall into her harness and took off. "This isn't so bad!" Marshall declared, dangling from Skye's chopper.

Suddenly, Skye spotted an eagle soaring toward them. "Look out!" she shouted. She made a sharp turn to avoid crashing into the bird. "I don't like eagles!"

"Wow, I didn't think the PAW Patrol was scared of anything," Alex said.

"Everyone is afraid of something, but sometimes you need to do things even though you're scared," Ryder said.

"If you can all be brave, so can I," Alex declared. "I'm going to the dentist!" He finally climbed down the ladder.

"Alex, could you help one last pup be brave?" Ryder asked.

Alex said he was happy to help!

When they reached the dentist's office, Chase and Alex bravely walked in together.

When their checkups were done, Alex and Chase told the
others they had learned how to keep their teeth healthy and clean.
"The dentist was super nice!" said Alex. "She gave me a sticker
and a toothbrush!"

The dentist had pulled Chase's loose tooth. She said a new one would grow in its place.

"I'm going to put this tooth under my pillow tonight," said Chase, "and hopefully the tooth fairy will leave me an extra-special treat!"

The next morning, Chase woke up to find a shiny new bone from the tooth fairy. He took a big bite.
"Oh, no! I think I have another loose tooth!" he said.
All the pups laughed.

BIG TRUCK PUPS

Adapted by Francis Xavier

Based on the episode "Pups Stop a Flood"
by Andrew Guerdat and Steven Sullivan

Illustrated by MJ Illustrations

The PAW Patrol pups love big trucks, so one day Ryder took them to a truck stop. There they met Ryder's friend Al, a trucker pup.

Al had an important job to do that day. He had to deliver supplies to help fix a leaky dam.

"Catch y'all on the open road!" Al called.

Al drove to the train station where Engineer Ed helped him load the supplies from Al's truck onto the train cars, ready to take them to the dam. Then Mayor Goodway arrived. She was in charge of supervising the repair team.

"Better get going," the mayor said. "There's a big storm heading our way."

There was no time to waste. Mayor Goodway got onto the train with Engineer Ed, waving goodbye to Al as the train speedily chugged away.

Engineer Ed drove the train as fast as he could. But part of the track ahead was broken. The train came crashing off the tracks! Engineer Ed and the mayor were safe, but the supplies had spilled on the ground.

There was a rumble of thunder as the storm moved closer. They needed help . . . and fast!

Luckily, Al had seen the accident happen in the distance. He called Ryder right away on his truck's radio—this was a job for the PAW Patrol!

The PAW Patrol gathered at the new Big Truck HQ in their cool new trucker uniforms.

"We've got to help get the supplies up to the fix-it crew at the dam," Ryder said. "I'll need Rubble and Rocky for this mission."

Ryder had a big surprise for the team—he was giving each pup a big truck of their own!

Mayor Goodway was relieved when Al and Ryder arrived with Rubble and Rocky. They got to work fixing the track right away.

Al lifted the train cars back onto the track while Rubble picked up the fallen materials with his truck's hook.

Rocky checked the train's engine.
"Uh-oh!" he said. "It'll take a while to get this train fixed!"

"The dam has to be fixed before the storm hits!" cried Mayor Goodway.

"Don't worry," said Al. "My big truck has enough power to ride the rails and pull the train from the front."

"Great idea," Ryder said. He knew that if everyone helped out and worked together, they could get the jobs done. "And the PAW Patroller can push the train from behind!"

"Now, that's what we truckers call a convoy!" Al said with a chuckle.

Ed stayed behind with the train's engine while the others journeyed carefully up the mountain in their convoy.

HONK! HONK! went Al's truck's horn as they went on their way.

When they reached the dam, more storm clouds were gathering.
Just then, Mayor Goodway's phone buzzed.
"Oh, no!" she cried, "The storm has caused a landslide on the other side of the mountain, and now the fix-it crew can't get through!"

Things were about to get much worse. There was a flash of lightning as rain started to fall, and then . . . **CRACK!** Water began gushing through a hole in the dam! "The water could flood the town!" warned Mayor Goodway.

Ryder heard the fear in Mayor Goodway's voice, but he didn't want his friend to be scared. "Don't worry," he said. "There's no way that Adventure Bay floods on our watch!"

He called Skye, Marshall, Chase, and Zuma on his PupPad for backup. They drove up in their new big trucks as fast as they could.

The team got to work right away. Zuma transformed his big truck into a boat, which he sailed into the reservoir behind the dam.
    Some logs had been bumping against the dam, making the cracks worse. He worked fast to move the logs away, stopping them from causing any more damage.

Before the pups could fix the dam, the flood got even worse. There was another **CRACK** when more water burst out. Mayor Goodway yelped as she was swept away by the water! **"HELP!"** she cried, grabbing on to a log.

"On it!" Chase said. He zoomed off in his truck, following Mayor Goodway. He used his winch to grab the log and pull her out of the water to safety.

"The mayor is safe, Ryder," Chase said. "But the floodwater's still headed toward town!"

Rubble quickly built a wall of rocks to send the water away from the town and toward the bay.

"Way to go!" said Ryder. "But we still have to fix the dam!"

The pups unloaded the supplies from the train cars to get started.

Rubble mixed cement, sand, and gravel. Marshall sprayed in water, making super-tough concrete.

Then Marshall sprayed the concrete into the cracks in the dam while Al, Rocky, and Skye worked together, lifting the heavy blocks to fill the gaps.

At last, the dam was fixed!

"You've saved Adventure Bay!" Mayor Goodway said later that day. She was happy to have friends who looked out for each other and helped whenever they could. "Thanks, Ryder and the Big Truck Pups—and your new teammate, Al!"

Everyone cheered when Ryder gave Al his very own PAW Patrol badge. Now Al was part of the team!

"Thanks!" Al smiled. "Just call me whenever you have another rescue that needs a Big Truck Pup!"

DARING DRAGON RESCUE

Adapted by Francis Xavier

Based on the episode "Pups Save the Baby Dragons"
by Sean Jara

Illustrated by MJ Illustrations

It was a beautiful day at Barkingburg Castle. The princess was leading the pups in a game of hide-and-quest.

"I have to warn everyone," the princess said, laughing, "I rule at hide-and-quest. Rescue Knights, are you ready? Ten . . . nine . . . eight . . ."

The pups ran off to find the best hiding places. Marshall accidentally opened a secret tunnel and zoomed down into the castle gardens.

"Nice! The princess will never find me out here," he said with a chuckle.

Meanwhile, Sweetie was avoiding hide-and-quest, taking a quiet walk in the forest.

"It's not fun when the princess always wins," Sweetie complained to herself.

Up ahead, she saw some baby dragons playing and gasped in surprise.

"Aww, baby dragons!" said Sweetie. "They don't usually leave the Dragon Highlands. I wonder what brought them here."

Claw, a former Knight of Barkingburg, and the Duke of Flappington, the princess's mischievous cousin, were nearby. They were hatching a plan to take over the castle.

"The trick to trapping dragons is giving them something they love, like delicious marshmallows," Claw whispered.

They watched the baby dragons fly over to the duke's wagon, following the delicious smell of the sweet marshmallows. The babies breathed their dragon fire, melting the tasty treats. They were too busy eating to notice the duke and Claw hiding close by.

Sparks, Claw's pet dragon, smelled the yummy marshmallows too and flew over to the wagon to eat some.

"Good trick," said the duke.

"I happen to be very good at training dragons . . . ," Claw said. He tiptoed over to the wagon and locked the baby dragons inside. "And catching them, too," he said, attaching the wagon to a harness worn by Sparks.

"Now that I have a herd of dragons, I shall take over the castle and become King of Barkingburg!" the duke said with a smile. "Let me drive."

"Fine, but we'd better hope the fiery mother dragon doesn't find us," Claw said slyly. "I hear she has quite a temper."

"A d-dragon with a temper?" the duke said nervously. "On second thought, Claw, you can drive. Bring me my dragon army when it's ready."

"Oh, no!" exclaimed Sweetie, "The duke and that naughty pup have taken those baby dragons! Their mama will be missing them! I'd better tell the princess what they're up to." Sweetie knew it wasn't nice to make anyone sad—not even dragons!—so she rushed back to the castle to get help.

"Oh, the poor little cuties," Skye said after Sweetie had explained.

"Their mama will be furious when she finds out they've been taken," said the princess. "We must help them."

"Don't worry, Your Highness," Ryder said. "No dragon is too angry, no pup is too small. PAW Patrol to the Castle Lookout. Time for a daring dragon rescue!"

The Rescue Knights assembled at the roundtable, ready for Ryder's instructions.

"Chase, use your dragon megaphone and tell Claw to stop," Ryder said.

"Knight Chase is on the case!" said Chase.

"Skye, I'll need you to put marshmallows on your grappling hook to lure the baby dragons off the wagon," Ryder continued.

"This puppy knight's gotta fly!" smiled Skye. Chase, Ryder, and Skye leaped into action.

The pups soon caught up with Claw, Sparks, and the baby dragons.

"Let the dragons go, please," Chase called.

"No way," shouted Claw. "I caught 'em, I keep 'em."

"Who's hungry?" called Skye as she lowered marshmallows with her grappling hook. The baby dragons tried to jump free, but their feet were stuck to the sticky marshmallow!

Suddenly, the harness attached to Sparks broke and the wagon started to roll down the hill. Claw fell backward into the sticky goo!

"Someone help me!" he shouted.

Ryder chased after the runaway wagon.

He notified the PAW Patrol. "Rescue Knights, I need you all for this rescue."

"We're on our way, Sir Ryder," called Zuma. The rest of the PAW Patrol were ready to roll.

The wagon was rolling down the hill, heading toward some fallen trees. "Autopilot, dragon wings!" Skye said, swooping down to help. With only moments to spare, Skye told the stuck dragons to flap their wings, which lifted the wagon over the logs blocking its path.

The wagon soared through the air, landing on the other side with a bump, and continued to roll down the hill.

All the noise attracted the attention of the mama dragon, who flew above, looking for her babies.

The PAW Patrol surrounded the wagon as it raced down the hill, now headed toward some rocks.

"Wrecking ball spinner on the double," Rubble called as he smashed through the rocks, clearing a path for the runaway wagon.

Zuma activated his launcher and aimed three buoys at the wagon, making it swerve and slow to a stop at the edge of a high cliff.

The angry mama dragon glided down and landed in front of the wagon, roaring and stomping her feet, which shook the ground. Suddenly, *CRACK!* The cliff edge broke away, and the wagon began to fall!

"Rocky, use your talon hook to snag the wagon," Ryder quickly called.

"I'm on it," Rocky said as he hooked the wagon, slowly hoisting it back to safety.

"Help! I'm falling!" Claw yelped, slipping from the marshmallow goo.

"Activate dragon net," Chase said, releasing the net to catch the falling pup.

"Oof," Claw said, landing safely. His plans were defeated, so he quietly sneaked away.

Once the babies were back on solid ground, Marshall got to work with his water jet.

"No more sticky marshmallow!" he said with a wink, hosing the goo from the baby dragons' feet.

Finally free, the babies flew to Rocky and gave him a friendly lick to thank him.

"Aw, you're welcome, little cuties," he laughed. It made him feel really good to know he had helped the dragons and that they weren't scared anymore.

The baby dragons were finally reunited with their mama, who gave them a huge dragon hug! *"Roooaaaar!"* she said happily.

"You're welcome, Mama Dragon," Ryder said with a smile. "Remember, whenever your babies are stuck in a marshmallowy mess, just roar for help."